Midsummer

Midsummer

a novella

Carole Giangrande

inanna poetry & fiction series

INANNA PUBLICATIONS AND EDUCATION INC.
TORONTO, CANADA

We gratefully acknowledge the support of the Canada Council for the Arts and the Ontario Arts Council for our publishing program, and the financial assistance of the Government of Canada through the Canada Book Fund.

We are also grateful for the support received from an Anonymous Fund at The Calgary Foundation.

Note from the publisher: Care has been taken to trace the ownership of copyright material used in this book. The author and the publisher welcome any information enabling them to rectify any references or credits in subsequent editions.

Cover artwork: Fran Forman, "Sailboat in Fog," 2012, mixed media, 20" x 20", ©Fran Forman. www.franforman.com.

Library and Archives Canada Cataloguing in Publication

Giangrande, Carole, 1945–, author
        Midsummer : a novella / by Carole Giangrande.

(Inanna poetry & fiction series)
ISBN 978-1-77133-138-8 (pbk.)

        I. Title. II. Series: Inanna poetry and fiction series

PS8563.I24M53 2014   C813'.54   C2014-902296-4

Printed and bound in Canada

Inanna Publications and Education Inc.
210 Founders College, York University
4700 Keele Street, Toronto, Ontario, Canada M3J 1P3
Telephone: (416) 736-5356 Fax: (416) 736-5765
Email: inanna.publications@inanna.ca   Website: www.inanna.ca

MIX
Paper from
responsible sources
FSC® C004071

For Brian

Part 1

1

OURS IS A FAMILY OF DREAMERS, beginning with *nonno* Lorenzo, who had a vision underground.

While my grandfather dug a subway tunnel in downtown Manhattan, his pickaxe shattered into brilliant light, revealing the shadow of a lost, three-masted ship. A vision revealed by the grace of God — or so he thought — a sign of blessing that flowered in Elena, his fortunate daughter; that grew in Eddie, his skeptical, educated son. Now in memory, I, his grandchild, peer into darkness, pause and hold my breath, witness my family born inside that flash of light, our shadows burned into the city's deepest stone.

2

L ET'S WALK ALONG THE RIVER, Adrian. Let's go back to our families' beginnings, to the spark that destroyed your ancestor's ship and filled my *nonno* with unaccountable wonder. His last surviving daughter has written us — my Aunt Elena, coming home to be with her kin. She's gracious enough to think of us as family; old enough to realize that she hasn't much longer to make what peace she can.

The Hudson River was once named *Muhhaakantuck*, the river that runs in two directions; that's my own family, toward and away from whatever blessing — real or imagined — might heal it. Here in New York City, we're strolling along a shoreline that was once under water. That was in 1614, when the Dutch vessel *Tijger*, weighted down with beaver pelts, sat at anchor at the mouth of the river, west of the island known in the Munsee language as *Manahatouh*.

Adrian, you know everything about this ship. Tell me the story once again, because when you speak, or even when you think of it, I can feel the wind of a chill day, and see its long shadow falling out of time, into that narrow passage where my *nonno*'s pickaxe is about to strike.

* * *

Dear Joy, I'll tell you the story as my father told it to me, in the Netherlands and then in Ontario, a tale handed down through generations. It's the gold coin that I brought with me from Canada, my slight bit of wealth, one that roots me in this foreign island to which my ancestor came. Watch the story come to life as I speak it — the Tijger *resting at anchor, not a large boat but a sturdy, hard-working one, a three-masted square-rigger, broad in the bow, built to withstand the ocean swells, armed with cannons to protect her cargo from piracy. Her seamen know that she is a source of coveted objects for the Lenape of Manahatouh, a band of farmers, hunters, and fishers; lately, traders with the Dutch who crossed the ocean after Henry Hudson's voyage up this great river on the* Halve Maen. *Gliding down that river from their day to ours, loaded down with bric-a-brac, the* Tijger *sails for the Van Tweenhuysen Company of Amsterdam, traders in pearls, wine, and textiles. Now its ships have come to the New World to barter for its wealth of beaver, otter, mink, and muskrat pelts, the abundant catch of the river valley.*

So we walk along this river of many names (North River, to the Dutch), where I imagine the Lenape hunters, bearing their pelts, making their way from the southern end of the island of Manahatouh to the Dutch ship Tijger. *A striking procession, long lines of tall men in robes pinned and draped at the shoulder like Roman senators of old, their deerskin leggings a protection from the cool air of autumn, their breechcloths adorned with beadwork. Others paddle canoes, great conveyances hollowed out of tree trunks, now laden with pelts, a small armada approaching the ship. For weeks the Lenape have been coming to the Dutch captain to trade for their catch. Before them he stands — a dark-eyed man, his pointed, well-trimmed beard accentuating a stern and wary look. With a captain's bearing, he is attired in a fitted doublet, a ruff at the neck, full breeches, a hat with a small plume. His name is Captain Adriaen Block, the man for whom I was named. I would like to call out to him across the years,* I know what is about to happen, how the story ends. *Yet he cannot hear me. I am not yet born, and besides he is a practical man with a deadline to meet. Autumn is sifting through the mesh of time and he has a ship to load by the onset of winter. He is meticulous, examining each pelt with care, paying each hunter from the ship's store of glass beads and buttons, hatchet-blades and jack-knives, bolts of cotton cloth, ribbons, mirrors, and pewter-ware. To this careful rhythm of barter and trade, the hold of the ship fills up with pelts.*

His deadline met, the captain must be pleased. As both an explorer and a businessman, he must expect to profit from this venture. Guilders, he'll have a chest full of them upon his return to Holland. Snow is gathering in the clouds overhead, January clouds. The ship is weighted down with cargo and, at this point, he may be thinking of his wife, of their house on Oude Waal Street in Amsterdam, of the gift he will make her of a warm fur; of his five children, the sons who will one day be seamen. Now it is time for the ship to weigh anchor, to begin the journey home.

They are about to depart when on the deck, the captain looks up to see a dark curl of smoke. He has no idea of its origin. He knows that on a wooden ship, fire could start in the hull, the keel, the rigging-masts, could end in a sudden conflagration, only he has no time to ponder these facts. Fire is hissing, flicking its tongue; flames lick and snap at the bow, crackling as they torch the foremast, setting the mid- and mizzen-masts aflame, collapsing the sails, shooting up through the great height of the poop deck while the captain runs aft, commanding his men to the dinghies from which the entire crew escapes to safety before the ship burns down to the water-line and vanishes into the sea.

The captain's load of pelts is gone. He is stranded in the New World.

If he wants to go home, he will have to build another ship.

No such thing has ever been done. Not by a white man on the island of Manahatouh.

* * *

There is a kind of enchantment in your story, Adrian, in the spell it casts, and yet it is a rather mundane incident, made exceptional only by the stories that weave our families together. No one knows how the fire started. It was an accident and there was no loss of life. History has nothing more to say about the incident. History tells us that Captain Block carried on, that he and his crewmen built another boat with the help of the Lenape, that he discovered and mapped Long Island Sound. Off the coast of *Roode Eylandt* (which he named for the ruddy colour of its soil), tiny Block Island bears his name.

A fire set by longing, is what you tell me, Adrian. I have never understood what this meant. Absent official reports, we may believe whatever we like about this fire.

In truth, this part of New York City has burned down more than once.

3

NOW IT'S MY TURN. As we walk, I am remembering *nonno* Lorenzo Salvatore, artist, mystic, and discoverer of shore-lines, a man whose visions continue to haunt us. Although I never knew my grandfather, it is possible that he is the reason why you and I met — or so my Aunt Elena thinks. His son Eddie — my father — did not believe a word his old man said. Yet even in death, *Nonno* Lorenzo is our keel, our hull, our family's rudder. We lift anchor under his sail.

A man of the dark, Lorenzo longed to paint. He left Italy from the crowded port of Naples, arriving in New York where dark towers gnawed at the sun, where he married, fathered children, wielded pick and shovel against hard earth tunnelling down from the Bronx, down Seventh Avenue, for the subway, through to the southern tip of the island until the light of *il bel paese* became memory in the blackness of the underground.

Nonno liked the foreman, an Irishman by the name of Kelly who even in the tunnels wore a three-piece suit, a pocket watch and chain across his chest (details that my father Eddie did not believe for a minute. *More of your aunt's make-believe,* he said, but it's true. You can go to the museum and ask).

James Kelly was a part-time vaudevillian and would have understood an artist like my grandfather because he himself had a fine voice and he sang underground as his men worked. *They're going to dig a subway to Ireland,* he sang because he liked his job, its grand vision in the dark below where in 1916, three hundred years after the *Tijger* burned and sank in Lower Manhattan, *nonno* and a team of diggers each took a pickaxe to dirt and struck a solid object. *Clear the dirt away,* the foreman ordered. They did, exposing the bow, keel and ancient ribs of a wooden boat. It was then that *nonno* saw light, a sudden flash, and against it the great shadow of a three-masted ship. He crossed himself. Then touching the keel, he felt the heat of fire.

4

THIS MORNING, AUNT ELENA'S LETTER ARRIVED. It was for this reason that we drove into the city, thinking we would like to collect our thoughts near the shoreline where our stories began. So we went strolling along the Hudson parkland between Chambers Street and the Battery, as if somewhere in those lush grasses and budding tulips we might also scavenge glints of meaning, some ancestral message that might help us.

Prim as a queen her letter was, shoved into the mailbox with the pizza flyers and real estate ads, so that you could feel its stiff formality, its smooth weight of fine paper, the past engraved in its return address — the Villa Borghese in Rome, where Aunt Elena lives with Uncle Carlo. I worried that it might be a death notice. Maybe a dead letter, a wrong address, a gala invitation posted during the Renaissance, making its way through six hundred years of Italian postal bureaucracy, finding its way to our door.

The postmark read *10 aprile 2000*.

"Looks like a summons from the Pope," said Adrian. "An excommunication notice."

"All it needs is sealing wax."

It seemed so odd, to receive a letter — let alone such a formal one — instead of an email. On the other hand, I could not imagine my elegant aunt tap-tapping at a keyboard. About to open the envelope, I felt Adrian grab my hand. "Wait, wait," he said.

"For what?"

With mock deliberation, he handed me a letter opener.

The envelope was addressed with a graceful hand, in fountain pen and ink. Its writing held the image of a quiet afternoon, French doors, an antique desk in a drawing-room, a woman attending to her correspondence. Aunt Elena was close to eighty and she lived without regard for the change of century, as if time were a newfangled invention. Her beauty was as delicate as a china teacup — one not set squarely in its saucer, one that a careless hand could tip over and break. A few years back when we took our kids to Rome, Aunt Elena's hair was still midnight-black with a comet's trace of silver, her eyes the startling blue of lupine flowers. Last year she had a ministroke. Now I wondered if she would still appear luminous, lit from inside.

"I wonder, too," said Adrian.

It was on our wedding day that the two of them met. When I introduced them, my aunt had looked bewildered, then reassured. "I was meant to meet you, Adrian Block," she'd said.

His eyes widened. "My pleasure."

"Our families are connected through the sea."

She did not have to remind Adrian about the seafaring ancestor whose name he bore. Besides, Aunt Elena no longer loved the sea. It was with some anxiety that she had come to New York for the wedding, to our reception at an inn by the shore. I still remember the look on her face as she spoke, how light passed through it as if it were a window streaked by rain.

* * *

"Are you going to open that letter?" asked Adrian.

Lost in thought, I had been staring out the window at nothing in particular. I slit open the envelope and pulled out Aunt Elena's note. The paper was elegant, the wording awkward — English stranded in the formal speech of her New York City girlhood. *Dearest Joy and Adrian,* she wrote. *On 21 June, 2000, Uncle Carlo and I shall celebrate fifty years of marriage. We were wed on nature's longest day, and it is therefore our wish to share its light with all of you … for nostalgic reasons, we would like to dine in that restaurant on top of the world.*

"She means the Towers," I said. "In that fancy restaurant. Right above where *nonno* worked."

"She seems to know the place," said Adrian.

"You think so? They never come to New York."

"With their bucks? I bet they do."

That's too un-Italian, I thought. Italians would never travel that far without inviting all the relatives for dinner. Yet of Aunt Elena's family, there was only my dad, and over the years, a cool distance had separated the two.

She's in outer space, your aunt, he would say (when he said anything at all about her). When I would object, he'd go right on talking. *With her kind of money, you can do whatever you like.* His resentment hurt.

Thank God for the ocean between them, I'd think, sensing the same ocean between myself and my father.

I have invited your papa, said Aunt Elena's letter, *so that we might gather our family once again.* It turned out that I had guessed right about her choice of restaurant — in one of the Twin Towers, gone now, high above the spot where over eighty years ago, grandpa Lorenzo dug subway tunnels for the IRT in Lower Manhattan. Along with living family, *nonno's* ghost would join us.

It is no coincidence that you met Adrian, she used to say. *My father would understand.* Yet when pressed, she would not say more.

"She's soft in the head, your aunt," said dad.

Everyone knew he had other reasons for avoiding Aunt Elena.

* * *

Dad maintained that his sister was full of nonsense. *Nonno* Lorenzo had been a labourer who had lived with his wife Maria in Brooklyn. She bore him five children. Their father was a peasant, he insisted — an illiterate man whose last encounter with a ship was the one that brought him to Ellis Island at the age of fifteen. *My sister had the good luck to marry into money,* dad said. *Like a fairy tale. So she thought up some make-believe to explain it.* Elena's tales had grown more elaborate with the years, he concluded. He worried about Alzheimer's.

I will bring proof of nonno's *vision,* Elena wrote.

I read these words out loud.

"You think your aunt's losing her marbles?" asked Adrian.

I fell silent. My dad would not stand for this visit, for its hard scouring of truth.

Adrian waved a hand in front of my eyes. "Earth to Joy," he said.

"Aunt Elena's fine," I replied.

5

A UNT ELENA WAS MY GODMOTHER, one whose gaze had always woven a protective spell, the vitality of her inner life flowing outward to embrace me. Her rich spirit, her family tales became our abode, the one that has sheltered our marriage and cradled our two sons. More than this, her words have given shape and meaning to our days, assurance that life itself is strong enough to toss a rope to a drowning soul, to rescue us from fire.

In my childhood, she and Uncle Carlo would often come to America. They would stay in some posh hotel in the city, then drive out to the suburbs to visit us in Beaches Point. She would bring me gifts — ornate Florentine dolls, tiny glass flowers, a fan made of Venetian lace. When I began high school, she presented me with a modern Italian grammar book. It featured giant graphics, bold colours, girls in miniskirts, and sexy guys buzzing around on cool red Vespas. It came with tapes. It was not at all my aunt's style.

"It is the newest way to learn," she said.

I had never studied a language. I wasn't sure I could.

"One day," said my aunt, "I would like you to hear my stories in Italian."

"But you grew up in America," I said.

"The stories grew up somewhere else," she replied. Aunt Elena explained that as a child, she had learned to speak both her parents' dialect and a refined, educated Italian — an achievement that puzzled her folks and delighted them at the same time. It was less a surprise to her father, Lorenzo, who had expected blessings, whose dreams promised him consolation for the loss of his beloved homeland. *Principessa,* he called his gifted daughter, as if she were Italy returned to him.

"Try to learn a little Italian," said my aunt.

"Is it hard?"

"Don't your parents speak it at home?" she asked.

My folks were embarrassed about their coarse rag-bag of Italian words and phrases.

It's only a dialect, said my mother.

"Listen to my story," said my aunt.

Once again she unspooled the tale of her youth, its shifting web that changed with every telling. As she spoke, the English words grew softer, more languorous, as if plucked and strummed and sung to a distant music. I was no longer sure what language I was hearing.

* * *

As a child, Aunt Elena had three older sisters, all married mothers. She was *nonno*'s youngest — along with Eddie, a late arrival, both of them conceived and born as her father aged and her mother grew weary of children. *Regali preziosi,* precious gifts, said Lorenzo, because they came *dopo il legno,* after he had touched the wood of the ship in 1916, after he had seen its ghost and felt its heat. A pious man, Lorenzo believed that his wondrous find — a ship on land — had to be a miracle, a sign from God. Just as he had left his native land by sea, so was the ghostly ship a reminder of his pilgrim life on earth, of his ultimate voyage to the world beyond, of abundant blessings that God would provide for the journey. For this reason, Lorenzo cherished his longed-for son who would bring honour to his family as an educated man, along with the daughter sent to care for them in old age.

Young Elena lived a dutiful life. She never dated. She worked behind the counter of Paolo's *Pasticceria* on Henry Street in Brooklyn, growing plump on sweets and fending off passes from her boss's son.

One day Paolo Junior shoved her into the pantry, fondled her, and ran off laughing. Full of shame and pleasure, Elena's heart turned into a hard fist and slammed right into the world. She could not breathe. When she calmed down, she cast her eyes on the contents of the baking racks — almond and sesame cookies, *biscotti* and *cannoli* — watching as they evaporated before her eyes.

Not knowing what to make of it, she understood that this was an act of supreme rebellion, that she had done this, and that if she could not undo it, she would be fired. Worse, they had an order to fill that afternoon for a banquet at Saint Anthony's church. She left for lunch, praying that Paolo's son would disappear instead. On her return, the shelves were brimming with fresh *crostata* and mounds of cookies adorned with sparkles and glazed with coloured frosting. Relieved, she delivered an enormous platter of sweets to the parish where the priest introduced her to the guests of honour, the banker Emilio D'Ottavio and his family who had taken refuge in the United States at the outbreak of the Second World War. The D'Ottavios were charmed by Elena's perfect Italian, by her courtesy and intelligent conversation. Elena could not take her eyes off their son, Carlo.

That night, Paolo's *Pasticceria* burned to the ground.

Dio chiude una porta e apre un portone, said her father. *God shuts a door and opens the front gate.*

Carlo did not forget Elena, and he and his parents came to visit. Six months later, the wedding took place, and soon afterwards, the young couple left America to begin their life in Rome.

* * *

Capisci? said my aunt.

Sì, I answered. Of course I understood.

"See how the story speaks to us."

In a language no one knew.

"You will learn Italian quickly now," she said.

* * *

My aunt was right. It was enchantment, the way that Italian fell into my ears, entered my dreams, took over the rhythm of my body. I studied hard, but it felt effortless. Italian was not taught in school, so I took lessons after class, convinced as I was that my aunt had bestowed this language on me from the bounty of her father's legacy. *Dopo il legno,* life had blessed us, also. My parents, stumbling over dialect words, did not know what to make of this.

6

ADRIAN SCRUTINIZED AUNT ELENA'S LETTER. "For the summer solstice," he said, "your aunt wants to meet us on top of a huge metal-and-concrete slab."

"Like Stonehenge."

"She's an interesting woman."

"I wonder if those towers are ... *aligned* with something."

Adrian looked puzzled.

"You know how Stonehenge is aligned. With sunrise, on the longest day."

"Your aunt would love that."

"Maybe she knows something we don't know."

Adrian got to work. A flip of the laptop lid, *click-click*, and an engineers' website appeared on the screen, a page crammed with arcane diagrams and equations. He scrolled up and down, looking bemused.

"No cosmic line-ups?" I asked.

"That tower was constructed at a twenty-seven degree alignment to the east of north. It sits on cambrian bedrock."

"Meaning?"

"Nothing. Just what worked for the engineers."

Those towers are gone now, of course, but in midsummer long ago, my cousin Leonora and I watched their skeletons rise into the grey haze. She did not believe they were going to be buildings. In the long days of midsummer, she saw them as fragile emanations, pure light. No, she wasn't a flower-child. She was Aunt Elena's child, which was more than enough.

I stared at the web page. "You Dutch are a no-nonsense people," I said.

"We try."

"I thought there might be an esoteric symbol."

Adrian the engineer put the laptop away, came over to me, let his hands rest on my shoulders.

"Ah, but come the solstice," he said. "A cosmic mystery will be revealed."

"Scratch my theory about the Dutch."

"I say it for you," he said.

And for Aunt Elena, who remembers all.

* * *

My sons were thrilled that their great-aunt was coming. They loved Elena, both of them — two young men who bore traces of her in the depth of their eyes, in the intensity of their presences. There the resemblance ended. They had their father's kindness, but also his precise habits, his clarity of mind — kids as bright as a pair of high beams, every neuron clicking. Jeremy was in med school, Luke was planning to study architecture, and both were as cautious as airplane mechanics who spend their days oiling machinery and tightening screws and calibrating all sorts of gauges, driven by the conviction that errors could be fatal.

"You know how they got that way," I said to Adrian.

"No, how?"

"I'll tell you how."

Adrian had not forgotten their childhood, when I had introduced them to Aunt Elena's Amazing Adventures — yes, like that, so they would picture Wonder Woman, the star in her crown ablaze. I had a tape of my aunt telling stories, and when they got older, I played it for them. They were enthralled and fearful at the same time. *Could I burn stuff down without my knowing it?* asked Jeremy. *What if I made you disappear by accident?* asked Luke. *Could I bring you back?* Afraid of black magic, they tried to reduce its power by fooling around with a few spells of their own. That did not last. As teenagers, they would restrict their disappearances to late nights out, and with time they began to notice the ebb and flow of all things. Older now, they worried about species extinction, vanishing forests, some deadly virus erasing the pencil marks of human life on earth. They got on well with their great-aunt, who held out the hope that nothing passed away.

My dad was never keen on my aunt's storytelling, certainly not to his grandsons. *Smog in the noggin,* he would say. *Thank God she's not here often.* Yet far from harming the two boys, the stories may have served as cautionary tales. Jeremy was thinking of becoming a psychiatrist, of researching what he termed Creative Hallucinography. Dad just shook his head over that one. Luke, impressed by vanished objects and fearful of species disappearance, planned to design skyscraper-greenhouses where threatened plants might reside. *I've got hippies for grandsons,* said dad. *I thought the sixties were over.*

Your damn crazy aunt. He said it to me, again and again.

7

THEN HE RECEIVED MY AUNT'S INVITATION.
"I can't believe this letter," said dad when I called him.
"Listen to this."

I was curious.

"'I have left the bother of a reservation to your still-youthful daughter.'"

I laughed.

"That's your aunt. Made of money."

"It's a special occasion," I replied.

"It's the biggest rip-off in the city, that restaurant."

"Hey dad, it's their treat. They're taking us out to dinner."

"Big spenders. Both of them."

I felt sorry for dad. Six months earlier, my mother Dorothy had passed away and he was grieving her loss. *Pretty Dotty*, he had called her. Or sometimes just *Dot*, like a period at the end of a sentence. Separated for many years, my parents had become friends again. Now I could sense dad's regret that he hadn't befriended her sooner.

"We'd love you to come," I told him. "There'll be lots of catching up to do."

"Yeah, right," he said.

"A night out will do you good."

I could hear dad's silence. I could hear him thinking.

"Your mother would've loved that fancy place," he said at last.

* * *

I called for reservations, then wrote the details in my appointment book. *June 21ˢᵗ. Midsummer. My aunt and uncle's anniversary.* The whole thing made me uneasy, prodding loose a stubborn clump of memory, an ancient diary, a bilingual entry. I dug it out and read it. *21 June/21 giugno 1971. La mia cugina ha telefonato i suoi genitori ... My cousin called her parents.*

I can still hear Leonora's voice on the phone. *Mamma, sono così felice ... I am so happy.*

Their last conversation. My aunt would have remembered that.

8

LEONORA AND I WERE FRIENDS as well as cousins, and although we were three years apart in age, we were both young in the careless time of pot and miniskirts and free love. We wrote to each other in Italian and our families visited in Rome. Both of us adored the Beatles, red-hot Vespas, and Marcello Mastroianni, so it might seem strange that we also fell in love with books and learning. We were passionate about history and languages, suspended in our own excitement like a blur of hummingbirds hovering over nectar. Words tasted sweet.

In time, our paths began to part. In my late teens, the allure of sensual language drove me wild, and a no-good tomcat on the prowl sniffed the air and found me. It wasn't so with Leonora. She lived a sheltered life in her Roman *palazzo*, and her parents sent her to convent school. Her dates were chaperoned. Chaste and gentle, she believed that one day the right man would enter her life, would explore with her the *terra incognita* of her own body. That was my best guess. She was too shy to talk about these things.

To be with her was to wander in a hidden garden, to imagine the erotic life of bees and flowers. Yet Leonora had a face of extraordinary strength and the erect posture of a Greek caryatid, one of those sculpted female temple figures that support the weight of a building on their heads. Perhaps this strength came from an Italian girl's instinctive protection of virtue —

how even in the sixties, a well-bred Roman nineteen-year-old presented herself to the world. It also spoke of determination, stubbornness, a refusal to bear a senseless weight that would crush her.

* * *

Having sent us the invitation, my aunt followed up with a letter in Italian.

I would like to make you a gift of one of nonno's *paintings,* she wrote me. *Hopefully, it will arrive before I do. There is no point in waiting until I have left this world. Disposing of one's effects overseas requires far too much paperwork in Italy. Don't worry,* cara mia, *it will make sense when you see it.*

UPS arrived with a large parcel, crated, packed and nailed shut.

"Must have set them back a few bucks," said Adrian.

"A few."

"And you said she had all her marbles."

We got to work with a hammer and crowbar, prying out nails.

"I'm afraid to look," I said.

Having opened the crate, we removed the strapping and styrofoam wedges, then lifted the painting out. I set it up against a bare wall, then stood back and observed it with care for the first time in years. The painting was my favourite of *nonno's:* an abstract study in indigo that became less remote as I gazed at it, as if it would repay deep attention with insight, as if one's gaze were a magnet which allowed its images, like iron filings, to swirl and loop and cohere. It revealed a face emerging from the blue patchwork dashed with glints of silver light — a woman's tender eyes, hints of warm flesh, pale lips. Her face seemed to hover, as if underwater, or floating behind a curtain of cloud. What made it so beautiful was its gradual revelation of form. *Nonno* did not impose his vision but allowed the viewer to bring it to life, as if we, too, were its creators.

The resemblance to my cousin Leonora was startling — the bright, gentle eyes, the set determination of her look, even the hairstyle, blunt-cut at the shoulders. It was painted in 1918, when *nonno* Lorenzo, in an artist's visionary state, had opened wide the veil of time to see his granddaughter's face. I could not imagine how he had done that, how years later my cousin and I would stand in admiration before the luminous paintings of an unlettered man. Even as a teenager, I had sensed an elegant and purposeful mind at work, one that did not suggest a humble, pious, illiterate soul who made his living with a pickaxe and a shovel. Adrian gazed at the painting, his look troubled.

"What do you think?" I asked.

"I — don't know. "

"You're surprised he did this. A labourer."

"I am."

"I was, too. Aunt Elena said that she used to sneak up and watch him paint. That's how she knew the work was his."

On our recent visits to Rome, I had given all of *nonno's* paintings cursory glances, not because they had become too familiar but because after so long a time, their profound stillness felt too disturbing, almost an accusation. It was true. Over the years, I had failed to attend to their wild scattering of light and colour that demanded and rewarded a viewer's stillness.

Realizing this, I understood what my aunt was doing. *Share with me the child I have lost. When I am gone, remember who it was that* nonno *saw.*

"The resemblance is so striking," I said.

"What are you going to do with it?" asked Adrian.

I paused, as if to gather up my strength.

"I'll hang it in my study," I replied.

"Are you sure that's wise?"

Your hands on my shoulders, more than touch: seismographers' instruments, moving over fault-lines, mapping cracks and fissures, sensitive to grief.

* * *

My son Jeremy hung the painting over my desk. It was just as well that I wasn't home all day. I teach Italian at a local college where I have an office, so I seldom spent evenings doing lesson plans in my study. Even so, the academic year was winding down and summer would find me at my desk more often, staring into the painted woman's eyes. It was then that I began to realize *nonno*'s potent gift, what Aunt Elena had wanted to transmit to me through his work. At night I would dream that I had walked through the painting's indigo waters, that at the call of Leonora's voice, I would be drawn into its depths. The dream recurred again and again. After a while it ceased to be a nightmare. Leonora's spirit walked with me. *Nonno's* unnerving gift of clairvoyance had brought her back to life.

* * *

By then I had understood that my grandfather had no need of an old ship's ruins in order to display his depth of insight. Like a reader of tarot cards, he had used an ancient symbol to shape vision into words. His underground discovery of the old ship was fortuitous, a lodestone, a coherent name for all that haunted him. Years later, the sea-captain's namesake came into my life. Perhaps *nonno* had parted the veil of time and seen this, too.

Yet I had to remind myself that my grandfather's paintings relied on the viewer to make sense of them, that no two pairs of eyes would share the same perspective, that I should make no assumptions. Whatever I saw was my own doing. God knows what Aunt Elena saw there.

9

ON JUNE 21ST, 2000, I WAS MONITORING EXAMS. While the students kept writing, I remembered a high school senior in 1967, her parents struck by how studious she was, her dad saying *you study too much, guys don't like that.* Her mom saying *leave her alone,* her dad yelling *she's my damn daughter, too!* And the girl said to him, *if I keep studying, I get to take part in the language competition and it's always crawling with guys, and there's money and a scholarship,* and her dad shut up.

In that year, hair down to my waist, beaded and fringed and a straight-A student, I was recommended for membership in the Saturday Italian Club at NYU. There was a guy named Rafe setting up the language lab, handsome and dangerous because he smiled at me. I had just returned from Italy and he said *welcome back, benvenuta;* then after our meeting, he asked me out for a coffee in the Village. I learned that his dad was a bank president, that he was the family rebel, with his own apartment on MacDougal Street, right above the cafe, in fact. No, he did not want to be a banker. He was going to be a travel writer, and he was already well-connected, having placed pieces in *Esquire* and *The New Yorker.* Hearing me speak Italian, he said, *you're well ahead of everyone here, college level. It's a pleasure to have you with us.* When I asked him what languages he spoke, he laughed and said, *a bit of everything, I manage to get by everywhere,* and thinking him modest, I was impressed. Handsome, as fair as I was dark, his gaze combined intensity and gentleness, yet a kind of introspection that hinted at some old wound. Such apparent kindness, a glimpse of frailty in a man — I do not know why it touched me, but it did. When he patted my hand, my stomach dropped into my shoes. He walked me to the subway, then kissed me on the lips, so that I almost fell down those cavernous steps, but that was not the worst of it because I was smitten, because the first mistake I made was to tell my parents about this nice guy Rafe whose dad was a banker, president of the same bank where dad worked.

A few weeks later, I qualified for the scholarship exam. Rafe was monitoring the written portion, the final section, and when I was through, he said to me *come,* and he took me home, and held me and kissed me and smiled. *Just so you know,* he said, *I get to pick who wins that scholarship.* I bristled. *I'm here because I want to be,* I said. *No one's forcing me, and I'll prove it.* I kissed him. He laughed. He was slow with his touch, and he murmured *I've never met anyone like you.* Slow, very slow, inside of me. *This can't be your first time,* he said at last. Only it was, I told him that.

I said I had never slept with anyone else. I was only seventeen. I had read a lot of books, and I wanted to know what it was like.

I hope you enjoyed it, he said.

I did.

He smiled and kissed me.

You're a good girl, he said.

* * *

A week later, I received official notice that I had been awarded the scholarship. The mail also brought a note from Rafe.

Congratulations on your achievement, he wrote. *You truly earned this scholarship on your own merits.*

I enjoyed our afternoon and your first pleasure. May you have many more such encounters.

* * *

I destroyed the note.

My own fault, I thought. *No one made me do it.* Even so, his arrogance knocked the breath right out of me.

My parents were thrilled with my scholarship. A few weeks later, dad said to me, *so what happened to that nice guy Rafe,* and I told him Rafe was just helping out with the Language Club and I was done there, and dad said, *nose in a book, you must have put him off.*

* * *

Still monitoring a college exam, I had drifted off in reverie. When lunch hour came, I collected the students' papers and left for home. First I stopped at a greengrocer's and bought a small bouquet of roses and babies'-breath. Then I drove eastward toward Beaches Point, the geographical feature for which our town is named. Just the Point to us, a mile-long wooded spit, its rocky fist jutting out into Long Island Sound. It is now a haven for birdwatchers, a nature preserve, a quiet place with trails, and a small dock with a limited amount of fishing. The Point was once very different, a ragged, unkempt patch of grasses, a booze-it-up biker haven after dark, a sex station for kids refuelling with a midnight swim in the buff. It was because of Aunt Elena and Uncle Carlo that it is now a place of tranquility and rest.

Cars are not allowed on the Point, so I parked at the beach, then walked in along the trail. I felt like a pilgrim as I made my way out to the rocks. I had come because of Aunt Elena, because of *nonno*'s painting, my hands moving along the rocks until my fingers touched the small plaque reading *Beaches Point Garden. This tranquil place is dedicated to the memory of...* I placed the bouquet beside the plaque, in a crevice between the rocks. Then I pulled from my pocket a photo of two happy people, Leonora and Rafe, and I kissed it and gave it to the water.

10

O N THE EVENING OF JUNE 21ST, Adrian, Jeremy and I drove into the city. Luke had arranged to meet us downtown.

"You okay?" Adrian whispered.

"Nervous," I said. He took my hand.

Luke was waiting for us in the tower lobby, and the four of us stepped into the elevator. It was a long way up, one hundred floors or so. Remembering Adrian's engineering website, I imagined that we were inside a huge astronomical sundial, shooting up the long axis of this solemn timepiece, like a whole pile of minutes on their way to nowhere.

At the restaurant in the sky, the doors slid open and we stepped out into clouds of iridescent glass, beaded images on a shifting curtain that covered a wall. It was as if we had entered into the deepest glow of summer. Adrian's bemused expression shifted into reverse and backed up into a tight squeeze of wariness. Our sons looked vulnerable and pale under the thin gauze of youth.

We're on Planet Elena, I thought. *Halfway to the moon.*

We were waiting for dad, and then the elevator doors opened on a downcast man who tried to smile, who blotted up light like an ink stain.

"Hi, guys." Dad grabbed Adrian by the shoulder, patted the boys' backs. He gave me a peck on the cheek. My father seemed lost here. He wore the look of a man who knows how little he counts in the world. Retired now, he never got his corner office at FirstBank in Manhattan, never earned the luxury of dining in places like this. The shadows of memory crossed his face, lodging in its hills and valleys of regret, his eyes that did not connect with anyone's. He slouched forward, hands in his pockets, eyes cast down.

Another elevator opened wide and out stepped Aunt Elena. She was leaning on a cane, her free arm entwined in Uncle Carlo's. Elena looked at me, and her eyes flashed blue, like a cat's at midnight.

"*Cara mia*," she said, and we embraced.

Over the years, sorrow had cast a fine net upon Elena's face, one as detailed as delicate cracks in porcelain. Yet her gaze had grown younger — innocent and stirred by light, like a day that has not quite dawned. She dressed as if she ruled a duchy — sapphires set in diamonds, black-and-silver coiffed hair, a draped evening dress of pale blue silk and a fine, white Pashmina shawl. She held the arm of her husband Carlo, a grave and handsome man with a silver moustache and a dark suit tailored to perfection. A hundred years ago he would have worn a sword and a bunch of clunky medals on a sash across his chest.

Dad grimaced, hands in his pockets, jangling his loose change.

Aunt Elena turned to him and embraced him. "Eduardo," she said. "*Mi dispiace.*" She was sorry about his loss. They had sent Eddie a Mass card when mom died. I could not remember how long it had been since brother and sister had seen each other. Then I realized that it must have been at Luke's christening, when Uncle Carlo, here for a business meeting, had brought Aunt Elena with him for the family gathering. Twenty years had passed since my aunt and uncle had crossed the ocean to be with us, although Adrian and I had visited them in Rome. Dad had not. He gave her a quick hug.

32

Luke and Jeremy stepped forward to embrace her. "Our future doctor and architect," she said. *"Piacere."*
The two of them were staring at her jewelry. *Aunt Bling,* said their eyes.
She caught their look. "Come with me to dinner," she said. Aunt Elena handed her cane to Uncle Carlo, and held out her bejewelled arms to Luke and Jeremy. They took them with the ease of gentlemen used to escorting royalty. What gracious guys. I smiled at Adrian, catching his look of bewildered pride. *Do we know these two?* his eyes said.
The maître d' led Luke, Jeremy, and their great-aunt into the restaurant, trailed by clouds of Aunt Elena's *parfum Dior*, followed by the rest of the family in single file. It felt ceremonial, a formal procession on top of the world. Every head in the restaurant turned. You could hear silent applause.

* * *

We were seated by a floor-to-ceiling window facing southeast, angled toward the East River and the Brooklyn Bridge. In the distance flowed an endless blue tent of sky that seemed to stretch across the haze of Long Island, all the way to the rounded edge of the earth.
"Che cosa meravigliosa," Aunt Elena whispered.
"So I booked the right table," I said.
"Below us, my father worked. His spirit is here, in the light." She spoke of the man who had loved radiant colour, who had spent his life working underground in the dark. I thought of his hypnotic painting, and I took that moment to thank Aunt Elena for her gift.
"It belongs to you," she said. "As if you were a daughter."
Silence.
Dad fidgeted with his napkin. "Hot day," he said. "You brought this heat with you?"

"It is the longest day of the year," said Aunt Elena.

"Do you know about Stonehenge?" Luke asked.

"I have never been there," said Uncle Carlo, "but I must tell you boys that on the day we were married, my brothers made a midsummer fire. It was after the war, and they could not come to America for the wedding, so they did this ancient ritual instead."

"You guys pagans?" asked Jeremy.

"The priest blessed it. He prayed that its light would shine forever."

"Look, and you will see," said Aunt Elena.

It was still daylight, and the sky filled the enormous window with a sheer blue curtain of air. Far below us, the gold-edged cables of the Brooklyn Bridge hummed with a brightness on the edge of sound.

Dad stared at his hands.

Part 2

11

M Y FATHER HAD ONCE BEEN A CONFIDENT MAN — a bank manager, a community leader in the suburb of Beaches Point, New York, a decorated veteran of World War Two. In his youth, he was fit and handsome, his rough edges of Italian masculinity sanded down to a smooth American grain. Back then the dollar rang like a bell across Europe, and when he would visit his sister in Rome, dad would purchase his suits and shirts and silk ties at the best rates from a *sartoria* near the Via Veneto. *I dress for a corner office in the city,* he'd tell my mother. *One day it will happen.* Only he was as restless as a night without sleep, and his hidden yearning was a cavernous thing, too big for any room he entered. I shied away from him. There seemed to be no space in the room for me.

Yet by then I had cleared some space of my own. I had been to Italy, I had become fluent in Italian, and by the summer of 1971 I had graduated college upstate with a major in languages, a minor in recreational sex, and a resolution to swear off men while I made a fresh start as a fellowship student at Princeton. Meanwhile, my cousin Leonora had been accepted into the University of Rome. Having been such a hard-working student with a deep interest in her American roots, she received from her parents a solo month-long trip to New York City as her graduation gift. *At last I am coming to America!* she wrote.

"Land of the free," my father said. *Out from under her mother's thumb,* I heard that, too.

I told him I had loads of good friends in the city who had studied Italian, who would love to meet her.

"I bet they're all bookworms," he said.

"Dad..."

"Now don't get me wrong, honey, you've got nice friends. But we've got to show her a good time."

Dates. He wanted to make the right impression on Uncle Carlo, his *molto ricco* brother-in-law with banking interests all over the world and the power to seat him in a beautiful corner office. He wanted to fix Leonora up, and he had a plan. Apart from his membership at the Outer Point Beach Club, he knew everyone who did business with his branch of FirstBank *and these are prominent people, honey,* like those he had met as treasurer of St. Anselm's Parish Knights of Columbus. *Our Knights and their sons are men of stature, which is what your cousin's used to.*

From the sound of it, all the well-to-do families of Beaches Point would know that we were about to entertain the eligible daughter of the D'Ottavio banking family of Rome. It was all so silly, so unnecessary, and I don't know why my dad was so insistent on matchmaking, on making himself look more than a bit ingratiating, if not foolish. Maybe it was nothing more than mischief, his wanting to prod and tease his strange and fretful sister Elena — maybe even a mean streak, knowing it would provoke her anxiety if the guy Leonora dated turned out to be a handful. *She's too damn strict, your aunt,* he would say again and again.

Then all at once we were two weeks away from my cousin's arrival, and not a nibble, not a single young swain hankering for a blind date with a super-rich Italian beauty, the brainy daughter of an investment-banking family. Poor dad, he was nothing more than a chunk of lint in the pockets of Old Money, but you could not tell him that.

Then he approached me. "What about that guy you used to date?"

There've been quite a few, I thought.

"Rafe," he said.

"We just went out for a coffee once or twice."

He doesn't want me to...?.

He did.

"Dad, he's over thirty. Much too old for her."

His clouded face was as quick with fury as a summer storm. "You're jealous. Two dates and he dumps you, right?"

"They weren't dates. They were..."

"Joy-less. Jealous Joyless."

"Cut that out," said mom.

"Cut what out?"

"Your damn sarcasm."

It shocked me, too, I had to admit. Sometimes dad would talk to me as if I were a sibling, not his child.

Dad paused, took a deep breath. "Okay, okay," he said. "I didn't mean that. I mean let's find her a big-brother type, someone to show her a good time. Is that too much to ask?"

My dad was so naive; it probably never crossed his mind that a good time nowadays might not be so innocent. Yet I felt sad for my father, beached on the shores of 1971 like a poor, disoriented ocean mammal, its sonar out of whack, too far from sea to find his way home. He had met mom through the church, on a parish boat ride along the East River. He thought weed was something that grew in your lawn. Whatever his own pretensions, he was sincere about hosting Leonora.

"Rafe's a nice, clean-cut guy," he continued. "His father's the president of First Bank."

I know, I know.

Dad's tone became kinder. "Honey, give him a call," he said. "Just do it for me."

* * *

I had not thought about Rafe for a while, and I had long since gotten over him. In fact, I have to admit to some stubbornness on my part, not wanting to oblige my father. A year after our brief encounter, I had received a letter from Rafe. *I owe you an apology,* he wrote. *In my travels, I've had much time to think over the harm I did to you. Having been through a rough patch in life, I've come to regret the hurt I've inflicted on innocent young people like yourself.* The serial nature of his offences did not surprise me. He went on to say that he hoped one day to marry, that he had resolved to change the destructive pattern of his life.

Welcome as it was, his apology could not undo the ache he had left in my body, the depth of my yearning for sexual love. I had found more men like Rafe, and now, for a time, I had decided to quit looking, to give myself some peace.

* * *

Recalling Rafe's letter, I wondered what he was up to now. I had read his articles in the *Times* and *The New Yorker,* following with interest his travels that took him far afield, to India and Thailand and Indonesia. God knows how much exotic sex he could squeeze in between flight delays or whatever, if he chose. He was a rogue, that guy.

Then I realized that I should not make too much of things. Leonora was not out for sexual adventure. If Rafe's apology was serious, he would want to prove himself a changed man. I would just have to warn Leonora to be cautious.

He owed me a favour. I picked up the phone.

"Joy," Rafe said. "What a pleasure."

He asked how I was doing. I told him about my academic accomplishments. He said he was living a quiet life that now included a woman named Elise, a steady friend.

Hesitant, I told him about my cousin.

"You're saying she needs a buddy," he said. "Someone to take her places."

"My dad's idea."

"Lunch and a matinee. A boat ride to the Statue of Liberty."

"That kind of thing," I said. "Your friend won't mind?"

"Not at all. It's so innocent."

I laughed.

"You know," said Rafe. "I owe you this."

"It's okay."

"Joy, it's not okay. I should have kept my hands off you. I should have just been your friend."

I hung up, dried my eyes, recovered my composure. Then I told dad that Rafe would like to meet Leonora.

"That's my girl," he said, smiling.

12

ON JUNE 9TH, LEONORA ARRIVED at Kennedy Airport, her dark hair swept back under a broad-brimmed hat, her blue eyes alight with a happiness that softened the determined set of her face. Running through the gate, she swept into my arms, kissed me on both cheeks and whispered "Joy, *carissima*, at last I have come." She was wearing a sleek, white pantsuit that still looked fresh after eight hours of flying. She seemed herself to be a kind of freshness.

"What's in these suitcases?" asked dad when we got home. I wondered myself. They were heavy, I had to admit.

"Books," said Leonora.

"You're kidding," said dad. "Reading on your *vacation?*"

She blushed. "Some are Italian books. For Joy."

There were other books also, she told me later. She was reading to improve her English while studying the history of New York City. There were novels for pleasure, in English and Italian. William Faulkner. Edith Wharton. Italo Calvino. No thrillers for the long, boring flight, not one. In her carry-on, a novel by Virginia Woolf. I was beginning to think that my happy-go-lucky dad was on to something.

I told her about Rafe. "He's smart," I said. "I bet he's read all the stuff in your suitcase."

"When will I meet him?"

The day after tomorrow, I told her.

She looked thoughtful. "I will speak to him alone?"

"If you like."

"That will be the first time in my life."

"You mean with a guy?"

She nodded. It surprised me to see that there were tears in her eyes.

"A man I can *talk* to," she said.

* * *

Poor Leonora. She told me how much she wanted to be friends with a man, to share her heart and mind with him before inviting him into the seclusion of her body. I sympathized with my cousin's wish, with the ache of loneliness that it revealed. Without mentioning my experience with Rafe, I told her that he was older, that he would show her around, that he had no expectations, other than keeping her company now and again.

I wondered if I should tell her that Rafe had a girlfriend, and I decided against it, a move I was later to regret. *I owe you this,* said Rafe when I told him about my cousin. *I should have kept my hands off you. I should have just been your friend.* As if I could move time backward to the day we met, as if his gentle treatment of Leonora would somehow restore my innocence.

I ended up telling her that she should be careful, being as lonely as she was. Loneliness was a terrible thing, and it could cloud your judgment around a man's intentions. She was only here for a month, and Rafe was not interested in romantic involvement. She told me she understood.

"But you do not have a man in your life?" She looked surprised.

"Not right now."

Leonora's gaze was sympathetic. "*Mamma* did not have this loneliness," she said. "Her family was together always."

I laughed. "And they had *nonno*'s blessing."

"Oh, you are going to take me to see…"

"Downtown?"

"Where he found the boat. Oh, please take me there. Yes."

* * *

We decided to make this visit on the day she was to meet Rafe.

"It's a construction site," I said to her. "You won't see much."

"It doesn't matter," said Leonora. "*Mamma* says *nonno* will be there."

Such sweet confidence, like a child in church. She wore a look of innocence, eyes uplifted, soft hands folding over each other like the petals of a lily. You could almost hear the clank of golden censers and smell their sweet clouds of incense. My cousin lived in her dreams, wrapped them around her like rich vestments. At times like this, it was hard to recall her devotion to study, to the intellect. She seemed so credulous, so easily led.

* * *

I took her downtown to the huge construction site near Greenwich and Dey Streets in Lower Manhattan, where in 1916, the Dutch ship *Tijger* had been discovered. Leonora was transfixed by the cheerful chaos of this place, by its racket of trucks beeping, cement mixers spinning; workmen steering backhoes, cranes and pulleys hauling dirt, the good masculine energy of buildings on the rise. Two days in America and here she was, oblivious to the stares she attracted from the hard-hats; childlike, almost incongruous in her flowered sundress and beribboned straw hat as she gripped the chain-link fence, wonder softening her face at the sight of cranes and winches and steel beams. It was as if she were standing before one of *nonno*'s abstract paintings that so rewarded a thoughtful pair of eyes, a quiet heart.

"*Che luce*," she whispered. She was staring ahead at a grey shimmering pole of light that rose and vanished into cloud." *Elegante,*" she said. "*Luce pura.*"

"It's not quite finished yet," I said.

"What is…"

"That's a … building. Two, I think."

"Above the place where *nonno* found the ship. *È vero.*"

A happy accident, I thought.

Leonora gripped the chain-link fence. "It is fate," she said. "I have come home."

Because we were standing on an island, I imagined us gazing out over the sea, then turning to watch these two grey forms, their strange fragility of arches and latticework unmoored as they drifted upward, hovering over the city. Mesmerized, I began to wonder what was in the air down here, as all at once I stood inside the noon of midsummer, in an unknown June when the elegant towers would leave no shadow, would vanish into light.

13

LATER THAT AFTERNOON, Leonora and I went to the Village
cafe to meet Rafe. From a distance, I saw him rising from
his patio table, standing and beckoning us over. Languid in
his movements, he made me think of a field of grain ruffled
by a breeze, as if we were the wind that had stirred him into
consciousness. The movement was so instinctive, so true to
his body that I felt his touch inside of me. It made an end-run
around my brain, got right into my skin and bone until the
quick judge of common sense slammed down the gavel and
yelled *order! You've had your turn,* I told myself.

Rafe took both my hands in his. "Joy, you're looking well,"
he said. Those eyes of his, what quizzical sadness I saw there.
He moved me still. "And this is your cousin?"

I introduced the two of them.

"*Benvenuta*, Leonora," he said, and he took her hand and
kissed it. "*Da dov'è Lei, in Italia?*"

Leonora blushed. She told him she was from Rome.

Polite, I thought. He had used the formal "you."

"*Mi dispiace,* I must continue in English," said Rafe.

"Oh, but I would prefer that," she replied.

* * *

Leonora's English was good enough for decent conversation
and awkward enough to get lost inside a sexy Italian accent.

Rafe's eyes were gentle. The two of them talked about travel, about languages and literature, supple voices weaving themselves a cocoon of words, enclosing each other in a space where I did not belong.

I felt a pang of envy. Once I, too, had been innocent, like my cousin.

I told them I had some errands to run.

"You will take pictures first?" asked Leonora.

I pulled out my camera. Rafe obliged and kissed Leonora's hand again. Then he posed with his arm around her shoulder.

* * *

"Such a man," Leonora whispered on the train home. "You think it will be all right, yes?"

I was not sure what she meant.

"He is so … intelligent."

I said her brains could match his any day.

"It is true." She giggled. "I have read every book he's read."

I asked her what they'd do for fun.

"He will take me on the Circle Line," she said. "To see the Statue of Liberty."

"And then?"

Her eyes twinkled. "We'll have ice cream. Maybe we will share a cone."

Two tongues licking a cone. Jesus. I told her that she must not send him the wrong signals.

"I would not do that," she said. "I am dressed modestly."

In my head, I cussed out convent school. *Is she really that naïve?*

It got worse.

"For the first time," she added, "I will try out a man."

Awkward English — at least I hoped it was. She made Rafe sound like a sports car fresh from the showroom, something you would take for a spin. Only Rafe was a used model, if ever there was one. I wonder if she realized that he had been around the block a few times, if it had sunk in the other day when I told her to be careful. While I was thinking this, Leonora squeezed my arm.

"I have made a mistake in English," she said.

At least she had registered my dropped jaw.

"'Try *to be*'," she said. "Not 'try *out a*'."

I asked her to run the sentence by me again.

"For the first time," she said, "I will try to be with a man. Without a chaperone."

I felt relieved.

* * *

"You kids had fun downtown?" asked dad.

Leonora smiled. "Rafe is very nice," she said.

Later dad took me aside. "I'm proud of you, honey," he said.

I asked him why.

"You've made your cousin so happy."

14

OVER THE NEXT TWO WEEKS, Leonora and Rafe became friends and constant companions — old-fashioned, chaste, platonic book-buddies. As Leonora described their afternoons at the Museum of Modern Art and their bookstore-browsing in the Village, I would sometimes feel a residual ache of longing, remembering my teens when I, too, had yearned for deep conversation and friendship with a man, regretting that in my case, the passions of mind and body would not be parted. Then I would remember that Rafe had a girlfriend, that Leonora would soon return to Rome, that this painful memory would vanish.

At the same time, I had just begun training for my summer job as a docent at a museum in Manhattan. Leonora would come into the city with me, where she would spend the morning exploring the museum and doing research on Italian immigration to America, especially to her mother's neighbourhood. She was excited because the museum would soon host a visiting researcher, a Canadian of Dutch ancestry who was interested in city artifacts, including the remnants of *nonno*'s ship. She wanted to talk to him.

At lunchtime, I would take her on the subway to meet Rafe. She was keen to learn directions, to be on her own in the city, and it was not long before she got used to riding the Lex, making the transfer to the F train, getting out at West Fourth, where Rafe would come and get her. After work, I would meet Leonora in Grand Central for the train back to Beaches Point. She would be waiting for me on a bench in the lower level near the entrance to the train, scribbling in a notebook already crammed with memories. There would be a sack of books from Brentanos at her feet, or else a wad of museum flyers and ferry schedules stuffed in the outside compartments of her Gucci bag. Her smile was dazzling. *Oh, I am so happy,* she would say, as if it needed saying.

It was the first day of summer when Leonora called her parents to wish them a happy anniversary. *I am seeing all the sights,* she told them. *Joy is wonderful company. And this man, a friend of hers who loves books, he is so kind.*

I could hear my aunt's voice. *I hope you are careful,* cara mia. *Always I have Joy with me. Don't worry, mamma.*

* * *

It was around that time that something worrisome began to emerge in my cousin. Nothing as banal as a crush on Rafe, which she would have, in any case, denied. The look of her began to unnerve me, the nakedness of a more instinctive, less conscious set of feelings; the strong, beautiful set of her face breaking apart to reveal a frantic creature trapped and caged and beating its wings.

A few days after her call home, she took me aside and in the tone of voice of an eager student, she told me she had learned something new.

How to use a diaphragm, I thought. No, I was being too sarcastic. Leonora was studious about everything; she was always learning something new, however mundane. Because our grandfather had helped build the subway, she had become fascinated with the city's convoluted transportation system, enough to puzzle out the underground map, to memorize the routes. Maybe she had figured out how to change from the C train to the Times Square shuttle. Maybe.

"Rafe told me that a woman can..." Leonora paused. "Experience pleasure with a man without going to bed."

Uh-oh.

Talk about knowledge deficiency. This was a learning curve as steep as Everest, which made me wonder what lesser slopes these two adventurers had already conquered. I thought of Rafe, after our first coffee, kissing me on the mouth at the subway entrance. Talk about tongue-tied, bad pun, but that is how the game started. From the sound of things, Leonora must have already rolled the dice and passed Go.

I asked her in what context this had come up.

"We were reading," she said. "Laclos. *Les Liasons Dangereuses.*"

Sheesh.

"You know, we are very close now," she continued.

"But Leonora, you..."

"No, no, listen, it is all right. We are only friends. I know, I am going back to Rome. Friendship grows large enough and the body starts to respond, it is natural. From there, who knows."

Who knows, is right.

She paused. "I am not afraid of my body."

* * *

I had never told Leonora that Rafe had a steady girlfriend, and now I felt troubled — with Rafe for taking advantage of her, and with my own naïveté. When he had spoken to me on the phone, Rafe told me that Elise knew about Leonora, that she understood the situation, that she would be out of town for most of my cousin's visit, which was now almost over. Leonora knew nothing. I regretted not telling her. It was too late now and it was my fault. My cousin had moved too quickly from the lecture to the lab, and what might have cautioned her a few weeks back would only wound her now.

* * *

We had good family times with Leonora, including a three-day trip to Washington, D.C., and Virginia. She was distracted enough by her love of American history to forget about having sex without having sex. Instead she fell in love with the Smithsonian and treated herself to an armload of history books.

On our return, dad received an invitation to an annual end-of-June poolside luncheon at the Spring Island Yacht Club, the most exclusive enclave on Long Island Sound, courtesy of Rafe's father, Michael VanDorn, President of FirstBank. Dad was thrilled. Mom and I were invited, and so, of course, were Rafe and Leonora. It seemed like a harmless, relaxing event, but a few days beforehand, my cousin took me aside.

"I will disgrace myself," she said. "I cannot go."

"Why not?"

"I cannot swim."

I had never met anyone who couldn't swim. I had grown up on the Sound, which means I've been enrolled in a school of fish for most of my life. We have gills on Long Island Sound. It's how we breathe.

"I could teach you," I said.

"I am not — *sportiva*."

"I don't buy that. Anyone can learn."

* * *

So I took her to a local pool and taught her. Basic kid stuff: dead-man's-float and dog-paddle, crawling and breathing, three evenings' work, but it got her on top of the water. Best of all, it was a cold-shower treatment for those steamy fantasies of hers. Leonora was delighted with her new skill. So was my dad. My cousin had not enjoyed the Outer Point Beach Club because she had been afraid of the water.

Elena's fault, dad grumbled. *She's much too scared of everything. Too strict.*

"Rafe will be surprised," said Leonora.

"Does he like to swim?" I asked.

"Yes, and he has asked me to the beach."

"You're not ready for the high seas."

"*Non ho paura.* I am not afraid."

I warned her not to drink alcohol before she swam.

At the poolside party, she demonstrated her new skills. Rafe never took his eyes off her.

* * *

Things progressed, I am sure now that they did. It was the look I saw on her face that should have alerted me — and always before a visit with Rafe. A creature trapped in a pretty, long-necked bottle, a frantic beating of wings against glass, waiting for deft fingers, the touch of his hand to release her. I sensed she enjoyed her entrapment for the moment of release it brought.

I had warned her about some things.

Not everything.

15

SHORTLY AFTER HER SWIMMING DEBUT — and with only a week of vacation left — Leonora told me she had promised Rafe something.

"You're going to swim across Long Island Sound?"

She laughed. She picked up her camera and thrust it into my hand.

"Come to the cafe," she said. "We will come in, and you will take our picture."

Friday afternoon after work, the kickoff to the Fourth of July weekend. It seemed innocent enough.

"Don't worry," she said. "In the camera, you will see two friends. That is all."

Fully clothed. I heard that, too.

"Carrying books?" I asked.

"Now that is a nice idea."

Rafe wants you to do this.

I began to wonder. Rafe had lived for years above this cafe, and he knew the owner and his wife. If a picture was all he wanted, he could have asked either of them to snap it. Or for that matter, a stranger who stopped by for coffee. After work, I went to the cafe, but I felt uneasy, gripped by a strange undercurrent of excitement. Then I got it. When they finally entered, it was I who would appear naked, clicking the shutter, I who had given my cousin to this man.

A big turn-on for him. Kind of a menage à trois.

It made me shudder. I had stepped into a trap.

I sat at a table angled with a good view to the back stairs from Rafe's apartment. When the two of them walked in, I faked it. I messed up the settings on the camera and disarmed the flash, clicking the shutter on a photo too dark to be seen by anyone: a young woman with disheveled hair who surprised me with a look of grave distress; a calm, smiling man whose gaze turned to honey in my mouth as he turned and kissed her, so that I could feel for a moment his tongue, his lips, and the ache of that first desire. I was the one aroused; it was my cousin who looked unhappy, humiliated by that kiss. Aware of this, desire fled as I put the camera down. I told Leonora it was getting late, that we would miss our train. She apologized. *Un minuto*, she said. She ran back upstairs to comb her hair and tidy her clothes.

* * *

On the train home, she was silent. I did not tell her I had messed up the pictures. I told her I didn't feel good about the fact that I had taken them.

"Rafe wanted a souvenir of our friendship," she said.

"You mean he staged the whole thing."

"I let him," she said, "because he had been kind to me."

I caught the *had*. Leonora stared ahead.

"I didn't expect that kiss," she said. "I have never slept with Rafe. And I will not."

"Did you want to?"

"I am too young. I am only … a beginner." She took out a handkerchief and dabbed at her eyes.

You've got to start somewhere, I thought, but I surmised that Leonora did not see the funny side of foreplay. I kept my mouth shut.

"You will have Rafe all to yourself," she said.

"Why would I want him?"

She looked me in the eye. "Today he told me that he slept with you."

I was horrified, that Rafe would violate my privacy, that he would use this fact to hurt her. To cut her off, was more like it. To turn her coach into a pumpkin at the stroke of midnight.

"It happened once," I said. "Four years ago. And believe me, I was not the first."

Silence.

"I will never make love," she said at last, "to a used man."

Part 3

16

M Y THOUGHTS WERE UNMOORING ME. Maybe it was the spectacular view below that did it, the sunlight that hummed in gold along the graceful spandrels of the Brooklyn Bridge, our dining table high above the place of *nonno's* real or imagined visitation; maybe it was all of these that made my mind so porous, so susceptible to unwanted thoughts. My dad, staring at his hands, mourning his lost Dotty — that, too. How I missed my mother, how I grieved for Leonora, for the loss of treasured things that do not last. Yet at our table, there was also present a kind of alchemy in the person of my aunt who, during my childhood, had sat beside me, spinning words into light. Old now, she had gathered us together, fine strands, the warp and weft of a great invisible loom, her hands weaving a thing of beauty, a pattern of relationships which she alone beheld. She was, after all, *nonno* Lorenzo's daughter, the keeper of an artist's legacy, and this was perhaps her final visit here. As much as anything, it was her presence that troubled the air, that brought back ghosts, that offered us reconciliation.

We had done so little to deserve it.

Aunt Elena put her arm around my shoulder.

"You are shivering, *cara mia*." She wrapped her shawl around me. "*L'aria fredda*. It is the air conditioning that does that."

* * *

The waiter came with menus. My aunt retreated behind the stiff pages and emerged with the knowing smile of one who dines well often. When the waiter returned, she caught his eye.

Dad shook his head at her. No one was ready to order.

"Beluga caviar," she said. "For seven."

Dad turned to Adrian. "I don't even know what that is," he whispered.

"It is our gift to you," said Aunt Elena.

Dad thanked her.

"Now Eduardo, you must tell me about your life," she said.

Dad looked on edge. "What would you like to know?"

"You have early retired, isn't that so?"

He fiddled with his linen napkin, shook it out, put it on his lap.

"Game of golf now and again. Fishing with my buddies here."

"*Buono.* You have a boat?"

"Yeah," dad scowled. "A twenty-foot yacht." *And I eat in a place like this every day,* his grimace said.

"Dad's teasing you," I said to my aunt.

"In fact we go fishing on the Point," he said.

I sucked in my breath. "The Point" was local slang. I hoped my aunt wouldn't get it.

Aunt Elena sat up straight, and looked right at her brother.

"And what is it that you catch at *the Point*?" she asked.

Dad shrugged. "Nothing you'd eat, *signora.*"

Aunt Elena looked stunned. Uncle Carlo frowned.

At that moment, the caviar arrived, accompanied by a savoury pear-and-potato *galette*. The gift included champagne.

Embarrassed, dad fidgeted with his napkin. "Great eats, sis," he said. He cleared his throat. "By the way, what I meant was you *shouldn't* eat what *we* catch."

Aunt Elena said she understood.

The waiter filled their glasses. Dad fumbled in his breast pocket, pulled out a folded paper, glanced at it, put it away.

He looked chagrined, but he smiled at his sister, a sad old dog's ingratiating look.

"I was going to make a speech, but…" He eyed the elegant first course.

"But what?" asked Aunt Elena.

"I don't want to hold up the food."

"The food can wait."

Dad raised his glass. "Your marriage was made in heaven," he began. "So it's only right that we honour you in the sky."

"How grateful we are that all of you have come," said Uncle Carlo.

Dad looked relieved. He raised his glass and his voice. "May you have many more happy years," he said. "*Cent' anni.*"

Aunt Elena's face wore the crushed-pink look of twilight.

"Speech," said Luke and Jeremy.

She hesitated. "*Grazie.* We have not *cent' anni*, but we have a blessing."

My aunt seemed translucent, lit from inside. Uncle Carlo took her hand. "I must explain that we used to recite in our youth," he said to us.

"Recite what?" asked Luke.

"Poetry, of course. We were taught to memorize in school."

My sons looked puzzled.

"Well, I see you do not learn poetry now, but your aunt and I still recite to each other. It lifts the spirits. So at our wedding, we recited the most beautiful love poem ever written."

"Now this poem is for all of you," said Aunt Elena.

I cannot remember where in the poem they began. Only these lines.

Set me as a seal upon your heart, as a seal upon your arm.
For love is as strong as death, passion fierce as the grave,
Its flashes are flashes of fire, a raging flame.

> *Many waters cannot quench love, neither can floods*
> *drown it.*

Nor can I remember where they ended Solomon's song.

Time and death, in their merciless passing, had, for a moment, ceased to be.

"This is our blessing," said Aunt Elena. "You see how much we love you all."

We lifted our glasses.

"*Salute,*" I said.

"*Proost,*" said a chorus of men: Adrian, Luke, and Jeremy.

Then I heard Leonora's voice, felt her tugging at my arm, and I wondered if this were Aunt Elena's doing. *Carissima,* my cousin whispered. Her hand let go of mine, her touch fading into air.

To you, too, Leonora.

"Let's dig in," said dad.

"*Che luce.*" Aunt Elena raised her glass toward the fading daylight.

Far below, the Brooklyn Bridge and the East River's lights were blinking on. Aunt Elena caught my eye, then held her hand up to her ear. In the distance I could hear faint music, as if she had set it in motion. Clocks and chimes and mysterious echoes; time striking the city like a bell.

Part 4

17

YOU ARE HERE WITH US, Leonora. I can feel your presence, so join us as we raise a glass. You live forever in memory, you have never passed beyond our reach, you fall on us in twilight still, as surely as you haunted us that summer when we lost you, when everything died or was being born, I do not know which. It is not always easy to distinguish one from the other.

* * *

On the Fourth of July, a week before Leonora's departure, Rafe asked her to watch the fireworks with him at Beaches Point. They would be joined by friends, he said. *Why don't you go with them?* my dad asked, but I told him I felt uncomfortable with the idea, like a fifth wheel. In fact I was still smarting with anger at Rafe's double insult: violating my privacy and wounding Leonora by telling her he had slept with me. I wondered why my cousin would want anything to do with him.

My dad, of course, never guessed the real reason for my reluctance to join Leonora and Rafe. He made other assumptions. *You think those two are serious?* he wondered, his pleasure edged with some concern. Rafe's father was, in effect, his boss, as well as a man with influence. Dad had not counted on either of the two falling for the other. If things did not work out between them, dad felt that he himself stood to lose when his niece went home.

My mother was growing impatient with this kind of scheming. She had heard it all before: how Eddie felt stuck and going nowhere, a modest, trusted suburban banker, a well-liked man who deserved better, who yearned for promotion, sure they would pass him over for a younger man. *What does it matter, Eddie? You've given us a good life.* She never tired of saying this when she thought there was no one around to hear them, when dad would pour himself one more drink than he needed. Only now she was saying something more important and she wanted dad to listen. She did not want his niece on a yacht with Rafe, out at the Point in darkness.

"Your mom's forgetting," dad said to me, "that today is Independence Day."

"There's no such thing as Independence *Night*," I replied.

"C'mon. She's safe. Rafe's bringing friends."

"Mom's worried he might get fresh."

"Yes, but honey, it's got to be the girl who blows the whistle."

"Dad, she's..."

"Rafe's got a boat," said dad. "They'll be on water the whole time."

Meaning what? I thought. *That it would cool them off?*

"It's not as if she could get away," I said. "She can't swim."

"Get out. You taught her. I saw you..."

"Dog-paddling doesn't count. Not after a drink or two."

"Don't worry," said dad. "I'll keep an eye out."

Dad had 20-20 vision. He owned binoculars. He had been a sentry during the war.

Certain things he saw with absolute precision.

Others, not.

* * *

I asked Leonora if she really wanted to do this. She hesitated. "Of course," she said.

"You don't have to, you know."

"Why? Do you want to go? Do you want an evening with Rafe? A chance to sleep with him again?"

The words stung, like the kind of dangerous insect bite that chokes the throat and closes off the breath. My cousin had pierced open an old wound, one aggravated by her presence: since that camera episode in the cafe, I had realized that I had never quite gotten over Rafe or given up his hold on me. That fact haunted my relationships with men and explained how disturbed I was by Leonora's trapped and frantic look.

I explained to her that I was angry at Rafe for discussing my private life. I wanted nothing to do with him.

Silence. "I told Uncle Eduardo that these people are too old for me," she said at last.

"Then why ... ?"

"Your father would be hurt if I did not go." She paused. "Rafe is still my friend," she said. "If not yours."

I told her I would drive her down to the dock to meet the boat.

That's better, her look said, as if I owed her that.

18

L EONORA AND I WENT DOWN to the Outer Point boat house
where Rafe had moored his yacht, the *Morning Star*. The
building was a spotless white clapboard structure, an antique
wooden ship's wheel on its outside wall, two brass lanterns
gleaming by the entrance to the indoor lounge. Long Island
Sound nautical chic; it spoke of quiet indulgence and an under-
stated luxury more familiar to my cousin than to me. Yet my
parents were members, and I hoped she would enjoy the place,
that she would feel at home with these wealthy folks, that she
might find some comfort with them after her disappointment
with Rafe and with me.

Only a few miles east of Beaches Point, this boat house
and dock belonged to the Outer Point Yacht Club. They
sat at the base of a landscaped, grassy hill to the south of
the main clubhouse, a rambling Victorian building massed
with rhododendrons and protected by tall hedges on its
west side from the screaming kids and flying frisbees at
the public beach. I had planned to drop my cousin off, to
meet up with some college friends for the fireworks on the
boardwalk, but I was beginning to think that I should stay
around. My cousin, out for independence, might need a
chaperone after all. For the first time in weeks, I thought of
Aunt Elena, and how angry she would be if she found out
what was going on.

A car drove into the parking space at the far end of the dock. Out of it stepped a couple, then another man and a woman.

"Looks like Rafe," I said.

The woman took Rafe's arm as they walked along the dock. Rafe glanced in our direction, then stroked the woman's corn-silk hair.

It surprised me that I felt nothing, as if by acknowledging my longings for Rafe, I had somehow chased them away. Yet you could almost feel a rumble in the ground, as if the earth might open and swallow Leonora. She seemed as brittle as ancient stone, about to break.

"This is disgraceful," she whispered.

"We can leave," I said to her. "You don't have to put up with this guy."

"But now I *must* be here. I must confront it," she said.

Not *him*, but *it*. This insult. I could not imagine how she planned to do that.

"Do you want me to stay?" I put an arm around Leonora's shoulder, but it felt as if I had moved right through her, as if she were as insubstantial as air. She turned to look at me, her eyes full of chill, offended dignity. Too full, as if they held the weight of generations.

"I do not need you," she said.

"If I'm there, it might keep things from getting..."

"I am not like you," she said. "Or them."

"You may not be," I said. "But you're my guest. I want you to enjoy yourself."

"I won't," she whispered. "As long as you are here."

And if I go, you'll have fun?

I never got a chance to say that. By then, Rafe and his buddies had made their way to our end of the dock. He greeted us, then introduced his friend Elise, tanned and svelte after two weeks of a California summer. She looked about his age.

Her hair was full of sunlight and it rippled in the slight breeze.

I should have told Leonora. Why didn't I warn her about those two?

I wanted to believe that Rafe had changed. I wanted to remember what innocence felt like.

No. *The opposite. I don't believe in innocence.*

How confused I felt. I had no desire to be cruel to her.

Leonora said hello to Elise, who then turned to me. "And she's your cousin?"

As if Leonora were a child, incapable of grownup conversation.

I told her yes.

"She's my good buddy from Rome," said Rafe.

Elise smiled at Leonora. "I adore Rome," she said. "We'll have a nice talk."

Rafe beckoned to the other man. Together they loaded a crate of bottles and a case of beer onto the boat, along with two hampers of food.

"You're going to join us?" Rafe asked me.

I told him I was meeting friends.

"We've got loads of food." He looked at me, puzzled, then glanced at his small group. "You brought swimsuits, I hope."

I decided it was time to go.

19

I SAW THE FIREWORKS, but I do not remember much. With my friends, with a crowd on the boardwalk that ran along the beach, I viewed Roman candles, pinwheels, shooting stars, the grand finale of the Stars and Stripes glittering against the black sky. As we headed off to the pub, I caught a glimpse of my father, a pair of binoculars around his neck, making his way through the crowds of shrieking kids.

He saw me and came over. "I'm going out to the Point," he said. "For a good look at their boat as they go by."

"Be sure to shout hello," I said. As if anyone would be listening.

"Once I make sure everything's okay," he answered.

What could you see in the dark? I wondered.

I checked my watch. It was ten p.m.

And if everything wasn't okay, what could he do?

* * *

Dad did not come home that night. Neither did you, Leonora.

After he finished lookout duty, he hiked back across the Point, a good mile, then headed off to the Outer Point boat house, where the bar was still open. He called mom and told her he would wait there for the boat to dock. When he hung up, the bartender took him aside.

"Excuse me, Ed, what boat you're looking for?" the man asked.

"The *Morning Star*," said dad.

"They put in a call to the Coast Guard. An hour ago, I think."

"Was the boat in trouble?" dad asked.

"Not the boat." He paused. "You want to talk to a cop."

I know what my dad must have been thinking. *Talk to a cop?* That made no sense. Cops are for bad stuff, like murders. This was a pleasure boat, owned by a responsible man, a banker's son. No way he would talk to some cop on the beat; he would only speak to someone in charge, a Coast Guard officer in crisp navy blues, gold bars on the sleeves, white military cap. Now the Coast Guard did drug enforcement, but not with the class of people who boated on Long Island Sound. Hell, there must have been some confusion. It may have been the wrong *Morning Star*, a common enough name for a boat.

He had only moments to think this before the police showed up.

***

The officer who came to the club happened to be a client at the bank. That put dad at ease, until the man told him that Leonora was missing.

Horrified, dad told the cop that he was her uncle, that he had gone to the Point to spot the boat, to keep an eye on his niece and her friends, just to make sure she was okay.

The people on the boat? A nice bunch. All adults. Rafe's over thirty.

My niece? Nineteen.

***

Only there was more, much more to this story, Leonora.

Dad was proud of his excellent eyesight. He still had his army binoculars, and once again he had to be a sentry, certain that if he could keep you in his sights, no harm would come to you. He would have fulfilled his obligation to take good care of his niece. Even my mother couldn't argue with that.

Only he was tired, and he wasn't sure if what he had seen had happened.

* * *

I imagine it now. I am haunted by my father's words to the police.

* * *

"They were on the deck," he said. "Lights on the boat, so you could see two men, three women. You could hear rock music pounding away. A hot night, they were in their swimsuits. Drinking, talking, laughing, yackety-yak. You could hear it from the shore.

"Rafe and four other people, my niece right there in her pink shorts and swimming top, leaning on the rail, cocktail glass in her hand. Had her in my sights. I must've looked away a second, turned the binos on someone else. When I checked back, there was a space where she'd been standing. Her glass was on the table. Empty.

"I figured she'd gone for a swim, so I headed back along the point, thinking I'd catch sight of the boat again. I didn't. I checked my watch. Ten-twenty. They were due home at eleven. 'I'll meet my niece at the dock,' I thought. 'Surprise her.'"

* * *

"Ten-twenty," said the cop.

"That's right."

"The yacht had a radiotelephone."

"Of course."

"I'm telling you, not asking you. Those people waited forty-five minutes before they tried to raise the Coast Guard."

* * *

No one knew why it took them so long.

"They took Rafe in for questioning," dad told me in the morning. "Cop said the guy was sure Leonora had gone in for a dip."

"Nobody *missed* her?"

"He said they'd all gone swimming off the boat, at one point or another."

"Yeah, but — "

"The boat circled around the spot. They looked for her."

"But they waited almost an hour," I said. "They must have been smashed. Were they smoking something?"

Dad looked shaken. "Cop asked him that," he said.

* * *

The police questioned me also, after the Coast Guard search-and-rescue dredged the sound, after they found your body.

Could I tell them anything about Leonora, they asked me. Was she prone to risky behaviour? Would she have been drinking or taking drugs? Certain that anything I said would be reported to my aunt and uncle, I chose my words with care. She had only just learned to swim, I explained. She was not one to take risks. In fact, I had warned her about drinking and swimming. I even told the officer that I had wanted to accompany her, but she was an independent soul and did not want a chaperone. I still could not understand what made Rafe wait so long.

"We're puzzled," said the officer.

"My cousin was a little shy. But..."

"Was she depressed?" he asked me.

"Not enough to do a thing like that," I said.

* * *

I was not lying. It was not depression that took your life, Leonora. You were much too proud to be crushed like that.

The scene is in my head like a YouTube video where you click on the arrow and watch it over and over — Rafe on the dock, introducing you to Elise, how in a moment you understood that you had always been a buddy, that there had never been hope of anything more, that against your better instincts, you had allowed yourself to think otherwise. In that same moment, your face once again became a statue's, the caryatid bearing the temple's weight on her head, the temple of family honour.

You had not slept with Rafe, but you had allowed him enough intimacy to unloosen fear, and then he told you he had slept with me, and then he introduced you to his lover. You were someone he had aroused once or twice. You were nothing more than an afternoon's distraction. He had to make sure that you — and his lover — knew that.

You went on the boat, and like the others, you changed into your swimsuit, drew admiring glances, had one drink, then another, even though you knew from my warning how dangerous it was to drink before a swim. You watched the fireworks from out in the middle of Long Island Sound, joined the conversation, nibbled hors d'oeuvres, waited for the music to get louder until you burned with the realization that Rafe had humiliated not only you but your family, that you had allowed him to do this, that you nevertheless had dignity because you belonged to the row of statuesque women who bore the magnificent weight of honour and its dark partner, shame. You may have intended to attract attention as you finished your third drink, dizzy with the conversation that went wheeling and swirling around you like a flock of screaming gulls; you may have meant to cool down in the water; you may have expected rescue, but we will never know. It happened that while my father had his sights trained seconds away, you put one leg over the side of the boat, then the other leg, then you slid right into the water and disappeared.

* * *

I had to go to the morgue with dad to identify your body, the image of it flash-burned into my eyes, knowing that forever I would look at water and sense that every part of it contained some part of you. Home again, I walked into your room and looked at your things: the tidy bed, your smart white jacket draped over a chair, your books on the night table. I felt that they were no longer real, that if I touched them, they would start to crumble and break like the desiccated clay of some ancient city collapsing into dust. So I sat on the bed staring at one of your books. It was in English, called A History of the Dutch in New York City, *and as I sat there, I heard my mother's voice.*

She was on the line to Rome, speaking Italian, and it was she who had to break the news to Aunt Elena and Uncle Carlo, and she was crying because she and dad had been entrusted with your safety, and they had failed to protect you. Afterwards, she hung up the phone and wept.

I, too, was in shock. I should have gone on the boat with you, I thought. No matter what you had said.

Yet you would have done it anyway. I know that now.

* * *

My aunt and uncle arrived to claim my cousin's body and her effects. We endured the funeral, then suffered their anguish and chill silence as if they had lost the power of speech, as if they, too, had died. They departed, Leonora's spirit left the house, and I grieved for the loss of the friendship we had shared. Lacking words in one language, we could switch to the other, so abundant was the richness of expression we had been given. All of it over now.

Nonno Lorenzo's gift was lost to us. Long ago, he and his crew unearthed a charred wooden ship, and that was all. *Dopo il legno* Aunt Elena learned beautiful Italian, married a wealthy man, then lost her beloved child. As in the end we lose everything.

20

IT MADE HEADLINES, my cousin's death aboard the yacht of a wealthy banker's son. Rafe had a good lawyer, and since drinking while boating was not an issue in those days (and criminal negligence was difficult to prove), he got off with a fine and a suspended sentence. Dad also had his name in the news (*"Uncle Failed to Rein in Teen,"* one headline said), and because of the bad publicity, he was, for a time, asked to take a leave from his job at the bank.

At home my mother, desolate and anxious, fumed and steamed so you could hear the lid jiggling on her silent fury. With dad out of work, she found a secretarial position with a life insurance firm. She had her own car, and one day she packed the trunk and the back seat with her belongings and brought them to the home of an obliging friend with an empty upstairs apartment. *I need time alone,* was the note she left my father. *Maybe the rest of my life.*

Dad did not try to get mom back. For days, he didn't move from his chair. Guilt played with him like a card-shark with a perfect hand, and the man broke down. When he recovered, Rafe's well-connected dad shuffled him off to a smaller bank — an hour's commute to northern Westchester, where no one knew who he was.

Part 5

21

THE SOUNDS FADED, the silver net of invisible chimes, the inexorable clockwork, *tick-tock, tick- tock* that marks our passage here. It was June 2000. We had survived a tragedy, we had come to the point where the brittle shards of our family life might be reassembled into a frail, imperfect whole. At least we could sit together at the dinner table, our toasts delivered with a measure of real affection, all of us eager to share a meal. Aunt Elena folded her hands and looked at me.

"Now we must talk about you," she said. "You are married how many years?"

"Twenty-seven."

"But you have never told me how the two of you met."

Of course I had. For sure she'd become forgetful.

"In fact, I have not heard, either," said Uncle Carlo.

Both of them losing it? I didn't think so.

"We met at the museum where I worked." *Days after the funeral,* I thought. *Days after you went home.* I was afraid to say more. That Canadian researcher had finally come, only Leonora was not there to meet him.

"Do you remember what I said?" asked Adrian.

I tried mimicking his accent. "'I have come to research the Dutch sea-captain, Adriaen Block,'" I replied.

"You should have seen the look on your face," he said.

Everyone laughed. Not me.

Adriaen Block — the name had made my stomach pitch and roll. Our lives had been haunted by this man. Leonora and I had grown up with the tale of *nonno's* apparition, and now a string of the captain's DNA had wormed its way through the door. Worse, it happened that days before her death, my cousin had been reading about the Dutch in New York City, and with great solemnity, she'd read me the Captain's story aloud. Maybe she had been praying, not reading. Hoping for some miracle through *nonno's* intercession, some form of rescue from grief.

Nonno Lorenzo told my mother all about him, those were her words.

He brought us blessings.

* * *

Of course we had told these stories before. Families do this all the time, dusting off their favourite tales, weaving and re-weaving them into newer and more resilient language, bringing them to life again for another generation. Yet a secret life hums under every story because we tell only what we can bear to tell, because this hidden life is the body's, open only to the beloved who we trust with our deepest hopes, our cries of desperation.

* * *

My aunt was not finished with her queries. "You both moved to Canada," she said. "Before you were married."

Eighty years old she was, and maybe a bit uptight about these things.

"A change of scene," I said.

"You did not finish your studies?"

"I took a break. Later I decided to become a teacher." Silence.

"And a mother," said Luke.

"Ta-dah," said Jeremy. Adrian laughed.

"There is no life better," said my aunt, in a voice close to a whisper.

* * *

My aunt knew all of this. It was ritual telling, a renewal of a common story, one she had heard before and perhaps had half-forgotten. Its repetition, like all the others, should have been one of the pleasures of a family gathering. Yet I had to stop there. I could not tell her how desperate I had felt as Adrian did his research; distraught, in fact, until one day I told him that my cousin had just died in a drowning accident. He was horrified, going on as he did every day about ships and water. I told her she was only nineteen, and then I started crying and I said that I would give my life to have hers back. He looked shocked, and I have to admit that my words surprised me. Adrian took my hands in his and said *but Joy it would not help to give your life,* and I wept. He said, *you must get away from here. Come to Canada, like all the other Americans.*

Draft resisters. I knew about them.

You have your own war, he said.

Having known Adrian for all of a week, I decided to move to Toronto, a city I had never seen.

* * *

I gave up my fellowship to Princeton, took a job at the university library in that strange city, and lived in student's lodgings in one of those narrow, brick-and-gabled houses so typical of Toronto, the room itself bare except for a desk and a bed. I lived in silence, answering my mother's letters with a word or two scribbled on a postcard. *It's okay.* Or, *I love you. Please don't worry.* I ate little, I lost weight, I felt so insubstantial that I thought I might dissolve into particles of dust. I floated through the city like a helium balloon that was slowly losing air, one that, in a merciful world, would soon deflate and break. Adrian was kind, inviting me out for coffee or to a movie now and again. A year passed, and on the first anniversary of Leonora's death, he took me camping in Algonquin Park. By then we had begun to sleep together, but I hoped for nothing.

* * *

Adrian knew and loved Ontario's wilderness. He came from the Netherlands as a child, then grew up in the southern part of that province, swimming in its enormous lake as if it were the sea. As a boy, he fancied the old Dutch sailing boats, and he kept a picture of Henry Hudson's *Halve Maen* on his bedroom wall. At night his dreams were haunted by a sinking ship, aflame in the waters of Lower Manhattan.

* * *

You were skilled at canoeing, Adrian, and it surprised me, how fascinated I was by the stillness of the water. Beautiful, the lake a mirror in the early morning, the loon's call rippling the air. It was this shivering sound that woke me on that first day in the bush, this cry of desolation, and so I rose before you, got dressed, piling on more clothing than I needed in July, even for the chill northern air — padded jacket, jeans and hiking boots. I walked toward the lake, thinking to find some wounded creature, then feeling the pull of a hidden hand in mine that would take me where I had to go, eyes behind my eyes seeing down into the deep serenity of the underwater, clear and lucid to the bottom, rocks and petals and ancient fallen leaves, carbon, like ourselves, until drifting into the water, I sank with the weight of a stone.

You came running in after me, you had been half-awake and watching from the tent. What the hell are you doing? you yelled, but you yelled it in your own language, and anyway I did not know what I was doing, I had let Leonora take me by the hand, I had been dreaming awake. I wept as you dragged me out of the water. You held me until the sun was high in the sky; you stroked my hair tangled with leaves and dirt. I cannot live without you, *you said, and I wondered if I had been sleepwalking, and you said,* you must let go of Leonora, you must wash her away. That is what you meant to do, yes?

You took a cooking pot from our camping things, reached over the dock and filled it up from the lake. You helped me remove my sodden clothes. Then you knelt beside me, took a cup, filled it from the pot and poured it over my body. I wept, my tears mingling with the water.

22

AUNT ELENA PUT HER ARM around my shoulder. *Tu sei scomparsa,* she whispered. *Dove sei andata?*

You have disappeared. Where have you gone?

Sono qui. I'm here, I replied. Meaning, *I cannot tell you where I've gone.*

"Back from Canada," said my aunt, as if we'd just returned. I was afraid she had been reading my thoughts.

From here on, she knew the story, excluding details about crushing guilt, about therapy. We returned to Beaches Point for our wedding, then settled in Toronto. While I was pregnant with Jeremy, Adrian got a job offer in New York. He worked as an engineer on the final tower in this complex, high above where *nonno* laboured long ago.

At that moment, dinner arrived — grilled shrimp with crème fraîche and aquavit, veal shank seared in parchment, pike with coconut cream sauce, a starter of Mahi-Mahi with Japanese seafood salad, served in a funky little crescent-shaped plate. Uncle Carlo ordered the wines, unfurling their silky French names one by one. I looked around the table, gazing at my family high above the earth, each of them transformed, etched in their frailty against blue sky like slight birds, and I felt a kind of helpless infatuation with everything and everyone. Maybe it was the wine, maybe it was the thin air at this stratospheric height, or maybe just my sense of gratitude that time had repaired my frailty as best it could, along with my aunt and uncle's sorrow. How grateful I felt for the love of Adrian and for my sons, for the beauty of the world around us turning into light. Surrounding us in our high tower was the longest day moving toward darkness. Knowing that this moment would not last, I rested in its ephemeral beauty, delighting in the tinkle of crystal, the bright notes of silver on fine china, the room's soft murmur of dinner conversation.

Leonora seemed to have left for now.

"Veal's fantastic," said dad. He turned to Carlo. "Is the food this good in Rome?"

"Rome has its own modern cuisine," he replied. "The next time you visit, we will show you."

"Oh, how I would love that," said Aunt Elena.

"So would my credit card," said dad. He turned to Luke. "How's the pike?"

Aunt Elena gazed out the window, her face touched with sorrow.

I wondered at dad's brusque remark, sure that he felt unable — perhaps unworthy — to receive this gift so quietly bestowed. His slight of Aunt Elena left me feeling pensive, and I could sense that Adrian had picked up the mood. He seemed far away, perhaps with Captain Block and his second ship, on which he explored Long Island Sound where now we live by grace of his mapmaker's gift.

In Adrian's distant gaze, I imagined the settlement of New Amsterdam, its stevedores unloading barrels of tea and spices from the holds of three-masted trading ships, the clank of rigging, the squeak of ropes and pulleys hauling freight down to the South Street docks. Now I ask myself if anything passes away forever, if my aunt's girlhood still hovered over the streets of Brooklyn to the east, mingling with the ghost of Captain Block, taking on tangible form and energy, like her shimmering confections of old. I thought of Leonora, of her invisible presence at the table. I wondered if dad's sorrow would ever leave him, if he would ever peel its bitter rind from his heart.

At least Jeremy and Luke looked happy. They were eating as if they always dined on *haute cuisine*, their stylish plates set before them, the sky as big as the sea against their backs. Thinking of sand and water, I remembered Luke's first trip to the Clam Shack at Beaches Point. Age six and as grave as a judge, he had stared at the bowl of steamers, then put his little plastic bucket on the table. *You have to put the shells in it,* he'd insisted. Cute as a clam himself. At home he had learned to put the shells in the giant ice cream tub, only big brother Jeremy was a mature nine and he used to say *that is so ugly, mom. Get rid of that thing before I ee-mul-si-fy it.* Now Jeremy was lost in meditative silence, gazing upon his plump shrimp in its buttery, translucent beauty.

"Sure beats your bucket a' shells, ma," he said. Everyone laughed.

"I remember you guys plotting," I said. "How to use mental power to make that bucket dissolve."

"So you two can make things vanish," said Aunt Elena.

Silence.

"Well — theoretically," Luke said at last.

"When I was young, I made things vanish and return," she told them. "It was because my father had a vision."

Uncle Carlo patted Aunt Elena's hand.

She turned to Adrian. "Did you know my father encountered the spirit of the sea-captain Adriaen Block?"

Adrian looked shocked. "No," he said.

He had heard the tale about the flash of light, the shadow of the three-masted ship. But that was it.

"And so you found your way to us," said my aunt.

"Then I have a lot to thank your father for," he replied.

Aunt Elena paused, her cheeks flushed. "*Nonno* Lorenzo found Captain's Block's ship. But the sea was no longer there."

"Guys see the ballgame last night?" asked dad.

23

L IKE A CHAIN OF FIRECRACKERS, conversations started pop-ping off around the table. Ball scores, stock market quotes, the ridiculous price of Broadway tickets, Mayor Giuliani's love life. *Damn mean,* I thought. The waiter brought dessert.

"A-*hem*," I said. The chatter stopped.

"Aunt Elena didn't get to finish her story."

"You have more?" asked dad.

"Yes," said Aunt Elena. "I have more."

I could feel the air stir, as if Leonora were listening. Even so, I realized I had taken a chance, drawing attention to my aunt's frailty. I hoped and prayed that her lack of clarity was caused by her antiquated English, and that all her marbles were stacked in a neat pile, none about to roll away.

Dad shrugged. "Your party."

"This," said Aunt Elena, "is the last story I will ever tell you."

Her voice had the bright ring of a hammer on a nail.

* * *

From her purse, Aunt Elena pulled out a yellowed sheaf of papers. She handed them to the two of us.

"What is this?" asked Adrian.

"Look at them."

Adrian spread the papers out on the table. They were the old and fading sketches of an artist — studies of a man with a pickaxe, short in stature but muscled and very strong. "*1916*," he read.

Dad's face went fog-grey.

Nonno Lorenzo had drawn the darkness of the tunnel, the splayed fingers of lantern-light, his hands wielding a pick, goring the earth. Then he had sketched his own perplexed face staring at what looked like a slab of charred wood, then his hands putting down his pick, reaching in to pull the buried object out. As he touched it, a flash of light threw against the walls a flitting shape, the shadow of a huge three-masted sailing ship. The last sketch showed Lorenzo jumping back in fear and crossing himself, and then a quick study of his face. His eyes reflected awe at a radiance that would vanish and yet never leave him.

"It happened below, to the east of this tower," said Aunt Elena.

"Who knows what he saw," said Adrian.

"Only God."

He looked at the sketches, then noticed the museum letterhead in the sheaf of papers.

"You have heard of this from Joy," said my aunt. "Here, read this letter. Read what it says. How *nonno* found your captain's ship."

Adrian touched the letter, as if it were a face.

* * *

Dad was aware that these sketches existed. He had just never admitted it, but now I remember why.

* * *

Now I can hear your voice, Leonora; what you said: I have *nonno's* stories of the sea-captain, I have his pictures.

Aunt Elena wanted you to share them with my dad. So you went to talk to him, but his Italian was pretty rusty, and to cover up that fact he laughed and said, you're too serious, you've got to relax for your big cruise tonight. *It was the Fourth of July, and from the stairwell, I could see and hear you in the living room, your silky hair falling forward from your neck as you bent over an envelope, about to unloop the red string from the fasteners, and then you looked up at dad and said,* I would like to stay home tonight.

He looked stunned. Honey, what's with the long face? You'll miss the fireworks.

I do not care to meet Rafe's friends. *You lowered your eyes, intent on opening the envelope.*

You're gonna stay home with a book? *Dad asked.*

Those people. They are too old for me, *you replied.*

You're mature for your age, *said dad.* And Rafe likes you. *He glanced at the envelope.* Tell you what. You go have fun, and tomorrow night we'll look at these.

* * *

Because I had overheard this, Leonora, I told you that you didn't have to go.

Your father would be hurt if I did not go, *you answered.*

* * *

In your effects, I found the large envelope you never got to show dad. Inside it were Lorenzo's sketches, the expressive face of a man with a pickaxe, but I was too upset to imagine what they depicted. When I showed the sketches to dad, he looked at them, then waved them aside. After the funeral, I gave them back to Aunt Elena.